For Amy and Mia
- S C

Follow your heart, and look after those close to you
- C P

LITTLE TIGER PRESS
1 The Coda Centre,
189 Munster Road, London SW6 6AW
www.littletiger.co.uk
First published in Great Britain 2017
Text by Suzanne Chiew
Text copyright © Little Tiger Press 2017
Illustrations copyright © Caroline Pedler 2017

Caroline Pedler has asserted her right to be
identified as the illustrator of this work under
the Copyright, Designs and Patents Act, 1988

A CIP catalogue record for this book is available from the British Library

Printed in China • LTP/1800/1649/1016

2 4 6 8 10 9 7 5 3 1

Badger AND THE Great JOURNEY

Suzanne Chiew • Caroline Pedler

LITTLE TIGER PRESS
London

"What a glorious day!" beamed Badger
as he played happily in the summer sun.
   "I haven't seen a cloud in weeks," Hedgehog
agreed.
      And the baby bunnies sang, "Yay for summer!"
as they splashed in the paddling pool.

The next day, Badger was mending Rabbit's parasol when Mouse rushed up in a panic.

"Badger!" she cried. "Come quickly! The stream's run out of water!"

"Run out of water?" exclaimed Badger. "Let's go and see!"

Rabbit and Hedgehog were racing down to the stream too. "Have you heard?" they called frantically. "There's no water!" "Fiddlesticks!" chirped Bird swooping down. "Whoever heard of such a thing?"

But at the stream, all they found was a teeny tiny trickle – just enough to fill Badger's flask.

"Maybe there's more in the pond," suggested Bird and she flapped off to find out.

"This won't last long," said Badger. "We'd better gather up all the water we've got left."

Back home, Badger quickly built a sturdy barrel.
"We've got a whole saucepan full of water,"
the bunnies called as they trotted into the clearing.
"And my teapot's full to the brim," added Rabbit.

But when they poured in everyone's water, the barrel was only half full.

"How will I water my flowers?" exclaimed Hedgehog.

"How will we fill our paddling pool?" wailed the baby bunnies.

"How will I wash my handkerchiefs?" squeaked Mouse.

"Hang on," Badger cried. "If there's no water left, what will we drink?"

As the summer sun shone down, the friends fell silent.

"Maybe Bird will find water," said Hedgehog hopefully.

But Bird had terrible news.
"The pond's dry!" she twittered.
"The frogs have lost their home!"

"That's awful!" everyone
exclaimed. "Whatever
can we do?"

"We must share our water with the frogs," replied Badger. Taking care not to waste one drop, the friends poured some into Badger's wheelbarrow and headed for the pond.

They arrived just in time.

"We're so pleased to see you!" croaked the frogs.

Badger picked them up and helped them into the wheelbarrow.

"Oh, thank you!" they ribbited,
splashing gratefully.
   "Perhaps we'll find more water
further upstream?" suggested Bird.
   "Good idea!" beamed Badger.
"Let's go and check."

But the journey uphill was steep, long, and very hot.

"I can't walk any more," sighed Hedgehog.

"We're thirsty!" wailed the baby bunnies. "What if there's no water left anywhere?"

"We mustn't give up," said Badger.

The friends struggled bravely on until, around the bend, they saw . . .

. . .WATER!
A cool mountain pool lay
twinkling in the sun.
"Dive in!" yelled the bunnies as
the others had a cooling drink.

"Do you know," called Badger, "I think these boulders have slipped. They are stopping the water from flowing downstream."

"But they're much too big to budge," chirped Bird.

"Maybe not," pondered Badger. "I've got an idea!"

Badger carved a branch to make a long, strong lever.

He wedged one end under the biggest rock and pushed down hard on the other end. But the boulder didn't move.

"We'll help!" called the rabbits and everyone rushed up.
"It's no good," twittered Bird. "It just won't budge."
"Wait for us!" yelled the frogs. And just as
the littlest frog leapt into place the lever shuddered,
the boulder wobbled and then it gave way!

WHOOSH went the water as it raced
along the dry riverbed.
"HOORAY!" cheered the friends.

Soon the stream was running again and it had finally started to rain!

"Your water catcher works brilliantly, Badger!" squeaked Mouse as raindrops dripped down into the barrels. "Now we can save water on rainy days."

"Hooray!" called the baby bunnies.

And everyone cheered, "Hooray for our clever friend Badger!"